Things We Left Unsaid
Copyright © 2024 Ema Brkic

Independently published.

Cover design by Ema Brkic

To anyone who has cried their heart out.
This is for you.

Ema Brkic

Things

We Left

Unsaid

And in the laughter,
all I heard was silence.

How do you expect me to live
when all I feel is pain?

I couldn't let my heart break again
when it was so desperately
still trying to heal.

There was an ache in my heart
so strong
I wondered if it was better
to not have a heart at all.

And in the sadness
there was a silence so sweet
it was suffocating.

It's crazy how someone who is
the cause of your happiness
can also be
the cause of your pain.

I watch
as I destroy my life,
slowly slipping
into insanity.

Perhaps,
I have been burning all this time,
unaware of the fire around me.

Only those
who wish to be saved
can be saved.

I am broken,
conflicted.
I am my own villain,
do not try to save me.

When people my age
were thinking how
they would live their lives,
I was here
thinking how to end it.

Perhaps in death,
I can live another life.
Perhaps in death,
I won't feel so alone.

My heart is a hero
but my mind is a villain.

I didn't invite my loneliness,
yet it showed up anyway.

I'll leave a rose
on your doorstep
so the rain
can drown out the colors.

You made me smile.
You made me laugh.
You made me feel seen
when I couldn't be heard.

In a world of chaos,
I longed for love.
But even something
as pure as love
was tainted
by this reality.

Love is an ocean.
You can either drown in it,
or choose to swim.

Is it so wrong to crave love?

two souls,
entwined for eternity.

When you live
in a cage all your life,
you learn to live
off of bones.

maybe,
in another universe
we were meant to be.

I thought this was for forever
but turns out
we were meant
to go back to
strangers.

I will always love you,
even with a broken heart
a broken smile
a broken laugh
for my heart is yours
even if it is shattered
if it is ripped apart
if it is drained out
if it is broken
if it is bleeding
so long as it beats
it will only beat for you.

my heart was already yours
even before you told me your name.

loving you
was giving you my beating heart
and praying
you wouldn't break it.

I can only love you in silence
from a distance
yearning for you touch
to hear your voice
for I know if I get close
I'll give you everything I am
only to be destroyed
by your love.

I did not meet you by accident
I know this for the way I felt
when I first saw you
how the butterflies weren't there
you felt right
a solace to my depression
a comfort to my loneliness
two souls destined to meet
entwined,
woven together
never able
to be pulled apart.

I will look for you in every lifetime
I will wait for you
even if it's forever
if it means we can be together.

I do not sleep,
I dream.
For you are the dream
I hold on to,
Praying
I won't wake up.

I'll never know your deepest secrets
or the prettiest lies
you hid from me.

loving you
was my biggest regret
for I gave you my heart
a fragile beating thing
and you ripped it
out of my chest
broken,
never to be put back
together again.

Oh to be loved and held in your arms.

I love you
with a different kind of love
the kind of love
with a passion
that would burn down the world
if it meant we could be together.

*I'd let everything in this world burn and
die so
you can live.*

I kept a blank page
In case you would come back.

Your presence
has filled my life so much
even my heart
has your name written on it.

If you were war,
I shall not know peace.
If you were an angel,
I shall not know sin.
If you were a rose,
I shall love your thorns.
If you were poison,
I shall drink it.
If you were wind,
I shall let you take my breath away.

We were a match made in heaven
but sadly we were stuck on earth.

How can I erase you out of my mind
when your name
is written all over my heart?

Do you still love the sky
even when it rains?
Do you still love the sea
even when you're drowning?
Can you still love me
even if love can kill?

"but it made you stronger"

I didn't need to be stronger.
I needed to be *loved*.

But what feels like a blessing can just as easily be a curse.

I wanted to believe it was love,
the kind that comes once in a lifetime
and slips easily through your fingers.
But it turns out I was wrong.
It was never love,
it was obsession.

You are my favorite memory
Yet my most beautiful lie.

And before I know it,
you're already gone.
Slipping through my fingers like wind,
only there from dusk till dawn.
Racing through my mind,
all the past we used to have
was all I've ever known
But now you're gone
and there's nothing left to remember
for it was like a fantasy until reality
kicked in
your soul is beautiful within
the world is cruel without
slowly I forget your face.
as I long for your embrace
you were my whole world
but where is the world if you're not in it?
Everyday I wake up,
feeling something is missing
in my head,
in my heart,
in my soul,

I feel empty.
Without you,
it will always rain

there will be no sun or rainbow
there will be no blue skies
there will not be a single day
when a tear is not shed.
I long for the past
but I know
this is something that won't last.
I lost it all
I lost my memory
I lost my thoughts
I lost myself
but most importantly,
I lost you.

Time flies,
time lies.
It is but a promise that erases.
It is but the truth disguised as a lie.
I never got to say goodbye.
All that's left is a sigh.
They say life is beautiful,
But how can it be if it took you away
from me?
I long for the nights I held you by my
side,
And the days we shared laughing.
With you gone, I live in what used to be,
Never being free.
They say time is supposed to heal you,
But how can it be if it just left me blue?
There is not a single thing that can fix my
broken heart.
Not a single word,
Not a single place,
Not a single person.
'Cause they'd all remind me of you.

Of how you used to smile, what you used to
say,
What you used to do, where you loved to
be.
Now our bond is broken
While the future stays unspoken.
There is nothing I wouldn't do to touch
you
again,
To see you smile,
To hear you speak,
To smell your sweet scent,
To hear you say "I love you."
Life took you away from me
And there is nothing I can do.
We used to be stuck together like glue.
Now the world is only blue.
It rains all the time
I start to forget the sunshine.
Time passes by and it fails to heal me.
How can it if every day I am slowly

forgetting
your face?
How can it if every day I am slowly
forgetting
your face?
How can it if every hour I wish the world
wasn't this sour?
Why is life sweet at the start but bitter
deep down?
Slowly,
I forget your laugh,
your smile,
the way you used to call me your flower.
You were my life
You were my world.
Now that you're gone,
I don't feel like I belong,
In such a cruel world.
The days pass by and I slowly forget the
things
you used to say.
Weeks pass by and I slowly forget your

voice.
Months pass by and I slowly forget your
face.
Years pass by and I slowly forget you.
As time continues passing by,
I slowly forget myself.

They say time is supposed to heal you
But it doesn't heal me.
It never hurts any less,
I just slowly forget about it.

I look into your eyes,
And get lost in eternity.
It feels like forever,
When I'm with you wherever.

I used to shine bright
Now I am fading slowly
A dying ember.

A final day comes
The light has gone from my eyes
I take my last breath.

But you keep your heart locked away,
In a cage always to stay.

You were my paradise,
But all I ever was to you
was a sacrifice.
You used to be my heaven
And you gave the impression
That you felt the same.
Now you're to blame
For you cut me
deep with a knife
And ruined my life.

But you made me wait,
In an unspoken paradise
And came too late,
So I stood paralyzed
At everything that could've been.
My thoughts were racing
At a blind fate.
You promised but you left me.
Now all is said and all is done,
There is nothing to hope for,
not even time.

Before you,
all I've ever known was sadness.
But you saw me.
You saw me and lit up my world,
Showed me light,
Shades of yellow,
Where there used to be grey.
Even though it was only for a moment
It felt like forever.
It really did.

After you,
all I was left with was sadness
and the memories you gave me.
Shades of yellow
became grey again.
And I was left
with this void in my heart
A hole where your love used to be.

But when I looked into your eyes,
I noticed something had changed
And it felt like we were strangers again.

I got my happy ending.
I finally got it.
I only wish it would've lasted forever.

Roses are red,
Violets are blue.
Once upon a time,
I used to love you.
But the roses have wilted.
And the violets have withered.
Once upon a time,
I finally said goodbye.

There's so much more
Beneath those tired eyes
And lonely soul.
A concealed beauty
That even the angels cried.

My happiness was right in front of me.
But of course,
Because I know I can never be happy,
I was forced to walk away.

No matter what I do,
It's never good enough.
I'm not good enough.
And I will never be enough.

You injured poor soul,
Don't you know no one is coming to save
you?

I wish for many things,
But of all of them,
I just want to be happy.

I'm sorry
for many things.
I'm sorry
I couldn't be
who you wanted me to be.
I'm sorry
I look the way I do.
I'm sorry
I smile the way I do
or the way I cry.
I'm sorry
that you had to know me.
But most of all,
I'm sorry
for being *me*.

But you see,
while you see the world in a bright way
full of happiness and laughter,
She sees the world through a tinted glass,
stained with tears and pain.

There's so much pain in my heart
that I forgot
what it feels like
to be happy.

I carry a scar for life
And it's my fault.
It's there to remind me
That no matter what I do,
I can't erase my past.

How I long for someone
To hold me,
Look me in the eyes,
And tell me
I am loved.

I long for you,
I think of you all the time.
I call out your name
and search for you day and night.
Only to know deep down
that you don't exist.

I love you
with all my heart.
And it is with that heart
that won't stop beating
so long as you love me.

If you were fire,
I'd burn in your flames.
If you were water,
I'd drown in your ocean.
If you were darkness,
I'd let it consume me.
If you were the moon,
I'd never look at the sun.
If you were a forest,
I'd get lost in your nature.
If you were ice,
I'd freeze by your touch.
If you were a match,
I'd let you light me on fire.
If you were truth,
I'd never lie.
If you were exile,
I'd walk alone.
And if you were death,
I shall not know life.

Until the clouds cry
and the rain
drowns me out,
My heart
only beats for you.

You say you love me,
Yet my heart feels empty
and my tears have dried.

I'm so tired,
Slowly I fade
Fade away
My soul
While my mind decays.

All this time,
I have been fading slowly.
Yet I have hid it so well,
No one seemed to have noticed.

And sometimes,
when the moon comes out
and I'm alone,
stuck in the dark,
I wonder,

Is it possible to feel heartache?
Is it possible to break your own heart?
Is it possible for a heart to still beat if it's
broken?
Is it worth it to love with a broken heart or
is it
better to never love at all?

And the familiar ache settles
in my chest
and suddenly I feel numb

and a heavy weight all at once.
I wish I knew,
If what you said was true,

For then I wouldn't have to worry
even if everything was blurry.

You promised forever
But that's a promise you can't make.
For you left me in the rain,
standing all alone.

I slowly forget your face
And long for your embrace.
Now you're gone
But you earned your wings.

You can finally rest now
while I'm left in the darkness,
Blinded by a light that isn't even there.

Slowly I fade away,

Wishing you would've stayed.
You promised me forever
But left me at *remember.*

I'm tired
Everything feels like too much.
With no desire
I drift from your touch.

I'm done.
Done playing the hero.
Being everyone's shoulder
to cry on.
Listening to other people's feelings
Just to have my own feelings
Ignored, buried inside.
And people ask why I've gone cold.
I've had enough.
I'm done being nice.
I've stopped caring.
It's all just become too much.

My whole existence
Is just a reminder
Of how despite the light,
I will always be stuck
in the darkness.

I could be in a room full of laughter and
yet I
would still find a place for misery.

Pulling me back
hard to keep track
of all those times
and so I wonder sometimes
What it would be like
maybe exactly dreamlike
and so I can only long
for the past
Where I know I belong
but it won't last
For the sweetness of life
disguised like a pretty knife
cutting deep
reminding me in my sleep
of those memories
to remember for centuries
Something gone forever
and out of my grasp
Slipping through my fingers
Like dusk from dawn
I miss it
how things used to be.

How much pain you must be in
To cry with your eyes closed.

I waited for you.
But you never came.

I am buried in my mind six feet under.

93

When I needed you the most,
you left me behind.

I need help. No one listens.

95

I just need someone.
I really need someone
who can make me feel
like I'm enough
And love me
for all my flaws.
I need someone
who can tell me
I'm worth it.
Who can love me
for *me*.

It's a different kind of pain
When you crave love
but have no one
to love you
the way you love them.

You say you love the sky,
but you're afraid
of the night.
You say you love the dark,
but you're afraid
of its emptiness.
You say you love roses,
nut you're afraid
of its thorns.
You say you love the rain,
but you're afraid
of getting wet.
You say you love to dream,
but you're afraid
of not waking up.
You say you love the sea,
but you're afraid
to swim.
You say you love the feeling of being in
love,
but you're afraid
to love.

This is why I am afraid,
when you say you love me.

I choose to love you in silence,
admiring you from a distance.
For in silence
there is no rejection,
Only the emptiness of words unsaid.
I choose to love you in isolation,
For when I am alone,
all I think of is you.
I choose to love you in war,
For in war
you are my peace.
I choose to love you in my dreams,
For in my dreams
you are within my reach.
I choose to love you in loneliness,
For in loneliness,
no one can find me but you.
I choose to love you in sadness,
For in sadness
you are the bittersweet melody.
I choose to love you in this reality,
For in this reality

you are the only world I live in.

And in my chaos
there was you.
Standing from a distance.
And I realized
You are perfection.
The only thing that seems to fit,
the missing puzzle piece.
A sliver of my soul
that I must have lost.
But now I have found it,
and it is you.

I choose to love you
from a distance.
As from a distance,
I fear no rejection.
I choose to admire you from afar
to see the smirk on your lips,
the gleam in your eyes,
the way you laugh,
the glow around you.
An angel from heaven,
sent down to heal what is broken.
To mend what can't be fixed.

So broken yet so beautiful.
So lonely yet so pure.
So miserable yet so loving.
A fallen angel,
stripped of its wings.
Bound below
by the cruelty of the world.
An innocent soul
tangled in the depths of despair.
Crying for help
but no one is there.
Tears of gold
tainting a divine face.
Slowly fading
as the light in the eyes dim.
Beautiful yet broken
by the corruption of reality.

Take me back to the first time I ever laid
eyes on you.
Before the heartache and the pain,
before I knew your name.

In a world full of colors,
you were a shade I never saw before.
Something divine,
something unique.
And my heart instantly felt
as if it was made for you,
Only you.

In a crowded room,
you eyes
are the only ones
I look for.
You are
the only one I see.
Even if
we were worlds apart,
you would be the first
I would notice.
For there is something
in your presence
that I notice you
in the ways
I can't for others.

No one compares to you.
I know this for I have seen an angel
before my own eyes.
Glowing in such a divine way.
That no one else
glows nearly as bright.
I have never been to heaven before.
Yet now I don't have to
for heaven
is right before my own eyes.
And if I go to hell,
I can brag to the devil
I saw heaven
in this corrupted world
full of chaos and despair.

Now that I have seen you,
I cannot make my heart
stop beating for you.
For you have stolen my heart
the first time
we locked eyes.
For you have stolen my soul
even before
we ever touched.

The stars may be beautiful,
the moon may shine,
the sun may be bright,
the ocean may be mesmerizing.
But nothing can compare
to what is right in front of me,
not even the angels.

I did not want this to be a memory,
I wanted this to be *forever*.

When is the heart not silent?
When it is suffocating.

I thought it was love.
But I was a fool,
to think you could love me.
For the first time,
I realized why
loving you was impossible.
Because your heart was never beating.
It was ice,
frozen to the touch,
trapped in the depths of darkness.

I told the stars about you.

Because you live in my thoughts,
I'm lost in them all the time.

Because you're out of reach,
I sleep a lot.

So I can see you in my dreams,
And pray I never wake up.

So I can look at heaven,
Even if I never enter it.

You live in my mind
Even if deep down in my heart,
I know we aren't meant to be.

For not even the ground
could chain you down.
Not even the stars
could shine as bright as you.

Yet silently I pray

That somehow,
You and I could still end up together.

"but you healed from it"

I never healed,
I only became more broken.

Being loved and feeling loved
Are two completely different things.

You could be loved by your parents,
Your siblings,
Your friends,
Your pet,
Your partner,

But that doesn't guarantee you feel loved.

So when someone asks me,
Whether I would rather feel loved or be
loved,
Don't be surprised when I tell them,
I'd rather feel loved.

For feelings are like fire,
The more you feed them,
The stronger they get.

Even if I know I am loved,

I want to *feel* it,
And not just believe it.

I wanted to fix things,
to fix my dying soul.
But I realized the halves of our heart were
different
and didn't click.
So mine stayed broken
while yours found someone else's.

I loved you.
I thought you loved me.

But I should've known
that your words were just words.
They never meant anything.

The lies kept on slipping from your
tongue
And I took in the poison,
Like a fool
Drunk on love.

Until I realized the sting
And how slowly,
You were killing me.

Of all the things
I thought I knew,
I never thought
it would be you
holding the knife
stabbed behind my back.

If loving you was a knife,
consider my heart stabbed.
If loving you was war,
consider me a soldier.
If loving you was fire,
consider me burning.
If loving you was silence,
consider me deaf.
If loving you was darkness,
consider me blind.
If loving you was with no words,
consider me mute.
If loving you was a crime,
consider me a criminal.
If loving you was a sin,
consider me a sinner.
If loving you was an ocean,
consider me drowning.
If loving you was heaven,
consider me an angel.
If loving you was hell,
consider me a devil.

If loving you was impossible,
consider me loving you anyway.

Nothing is louder
than the silence
between two people
who used to be in love.

No one told me
The violence and pain
It takes
To become so broken,
So fragile.

That even the smallest word
Can break your heart.

When you are not loved properly,
You learn to take it for granted
The first chance you get.

But then you realize
How easily you can lose it.
How fragile love is.
How ruined it is,
Yet somehow still beautiful,
Worthwhile.

And then you ask yourself,
Why people love so fiercely,
knowing they will intentionally end up
Hurting themselves.

You used to walk beside me
And I would hold your hand.
But that used to be,
And I still don't understand

Why life took you away,
For now I only have memories,
And I wish you'd stay.
I promise I'll remember you for centuries.

Now I'm left all alone
Staring at nothing at all.
You were the only thing I've ever known
And now I feel so small.

You said you wouldn't leave
But you left me to grieve.

My heart may be broken,
My heart may be torn,
My heart may be rotten,
My heart may be cold.

But it is still beating
And longing for love.

The kind that comes once into your life
And lingers forever.

The kind that is a light in the darkness
And makes the shadows disappear.

My heart is fragile
My heart is bleeding
Yet still alive
And beating.

However my heart may be,
Just know this -
It is *yours*.

How lovely it must be
To be in love
And have someone
Who loves you back.

To be at ease,
to feel the absence of butterflies.

To be at comfort,
happy even when there's no reason to be.

A burning passion,
turning the waves of the ocean.

A flicker of a candlelight,
illuminating the darkness.

A sea of currents,
carrying me to shore.

How lovely it must be,
To be in love.

How miserable it must be,
For it to just be a dream.

Because I can't have you,
I look up at the stars.

Because I know,
At least we'll be staring at the same sky.

ACKNOWLEDGEMENTS

This book has been a long journey filled with my own random thoughts. It started off as just things I would think of, but I ended up wanting to share it.

Life is full of ups and downs, good and bad, so I especially wanted to highlight the beauty of love but also the inevitable pain it comes from loving.

Thanks to Kittl for the cover template.

Thank you to my parents, Patricia and Dario Brkic, for always supporting me and being there for me through thick and thin - you have never judged me regardless of what was going on in my life and for that I am forever grateful. I love you both.

Thank you also to my sister, Nora Brkic, my role model, who I look up to everyday and can talk to about anything - the world wouldn't be the same without you.

Lastly, I would like to thank you, reader, for choosing to pick up this book and give it a chance - this book wouldn't be what it was without you.

About the Author

Ema Brkic was born in South Korea and has been living there her whole life. She attends an international school there and is currently in high school. This is her first novel. She loves literature, reading, writing, baking, and especially writing her own poetry and stories. Her all-time favorite book series are the Cruel Prince and Once Upon A Broken Heart. She is a huge fan of dark fantasy and romance book genres. She lives with her parents and Siberian Husky, Loki, who she loves a lot. She has an older sister currently attending college.